# RESPECT YOUR PET!

## NATASHA SUMMER SAUVE

# Foreword

Pets are more than just companions; they are family. They teach us about love, responsibility, and the joy of friendship. "RESPECT your Pet!" is a heartfelt story that captures the beauty of learning how to care for a pet properly and understanding their needs. Inspired by the journey of a family welcoming a puppy named Oliver, this book is a delightful adventure filled with lessons about respect, patience, and unconditional love.

# Dedication

To my wonderful sons and their adorable puppy, Oliver. You have brought so much love and joy into our lives, and watching your friendship grow has been the inspiration for this story. May your days be filled with laughter, learning, and the happiest puppy snuggles and secret licks.

# Acknowledgement

I want to express my deepest gratitude to my amazing children, whose boundless curiosity and love for animals have been the driving force behind this book. Your enthusiasm, imagination, and the joy you bring to our home made every word of this story come to life. Watching you care for Oliver with kindness and excitement has been my greatest inspiration. Thank you for reminding me daily of the beauty in learning, growing, and loving wholeheartedly.

# About the Author

As an Early Childhood Educator with years of experience and a proud mom to two wonderful boys, I've spent countless hours immersed in the magic of stories. Circle Time was always a cherished part of my day—watching the children's faces light up as we journeyed through books together was truly rewarding. At home, reading bedtime stories to my sons became a nightly ritual, fostering connection and sparking their imaginations.

These moments, filled with laughter, curiosity, and learning, taught me the profound impact that stories have on young minds. Over the years, I've discovered what captivates children, what resonates with them, and what makes them giggle with delight. Writing books stems from my passion for creating stories that not only entertain but also offer meaningful connections for little readers. For me, reading isn't just about the words on the page—it's about opening doors to a world where children see themselves, their experiences, and their limitless possibilities.

# Moral of the Story

Caring for a pet is more than just fun and games—it's a commitment to love, respect, and responsibility. Every animal has their own personality, needs, and ways of expressing themselves. When we listen and understand them, we build stronger, more meaningful bonds.

# Authors Notes

Writing this book has been a journey filled with heartwarming moments. Pets teach us valuable lessons about patience, kindness, and the importance of responsibility. I hope this story brings joy to every reader and encourages young minds to treat animals with love and respect.

I 've got news that 's happy and bright,
Our family got a new pup tonight!
A sweet little puppy, we 've named him Ollie,
And he looks so dashing in his new blue collie.

When Mom brought him home, I cried joyful tears,
I 've loved him already for years and years!
I want to cuddle him all night and all day,
I 'd never let anyone take him away!

From the start, he became my best mate,
I promised to love him; it must be fate!
I swore I'd protect him from every big scare,
So, I packed him up and took him everywhere.

I watched him snooze, so peaceful and sweet,
And followed him 'round on his tiny, quick feet.
Whether awake or asleep, for his sake,
I was by his side—I never took a break!

Soon our routine felt a bit stale,
So, I set out with Ollie to try a new trail.

I thought a hike would be such a delight,
So, I grabbed my bike, but Ollie took flight!

Ollie wasn't thrilled, I must say,
He ran off in a hurry, zoomed away!

It turns out hiking wasn't his scene,
So, I thought, "Let's bounce on the trampoline!"
But my brother cried, "That's unsafe mean!"

I 'd never want my puppy to get hurt,
So, I knew right away my plan wouldn 't work.

Next, I popped on some shades and a hat,
But Ollie said "Nope, I 'm not wearing that!"
So, I grabbed little boots and a superhero cape,
We were scheming together our daring escape.

But Ollie wasn 't thrilled with my stylish spree,
He bolted away, as quick as could be!

But giving up just isn 't my style,
I love my pup; he makes me smile!
I thought he'd enjoy a game called Vet,
So, I grabbed my doctor bag—my best one yet.

I tried to check why his tail wags,
With bandages, tools, and pretend dog tags.
"Hold still," I said, to ensure he was fine,
But off he ran, not a patient of mine!

Since he didn't enjoy my medical feature,
I decided to cancel his next procedure.

My puppy's always right at my feet,
Whenever my family sits down to eat.
I think he's craving something new,
And I know just what I can do!

To make my little Ollie glad,
I shared some snacks that I had.
He gobbled it up in a single sup,
I'm so proud of my sweet little pup!

The very next morning, what did we see?
Some poop on the floor—it was left by Ollie!
Then Dad yelled out, "Oh no, there's four more!"
Our poor little pup had a stomach that's sore.

The food I had shared gave him quite an ache,
So, I rushed to tell Mom for Ollies sake.
She called up the vet, explained the ordeal,
And soon we found out he'd completely heal.

Now I 've learned that for my pup to eat,
It 's got to be a proper doggy treat!

I was feeling a bit down, so I sat on my swing,
When suddenly, I thought of the perfect thing!

I remembered a toy I'd bought from the store,
A squeaky chicken that Ollie would adore!

I called him to play, and what a delight,
The chicken's squeak made his eyes shine bright!

I tossed the chicken way up high,
He leapt and caught it, oh my, oh my!

At last, I 'd found a game he truly loved,
No more bike rides; this fit him like a glove!

My puppy is such a sweet little boy,
But I 've learned he 's more than just a toy.

Puppies love to run, walk, and fetch,
And mine even has a big sweet stretch!

So instead of treating him like a doll,
We play all day with his favorite ball.

I 've learned what 's safe for him to eat,
And no more sneaking snacks from under my feet!

My mommy says with love and care,
He 'll always be my fluffy teddy bear.